D0573911

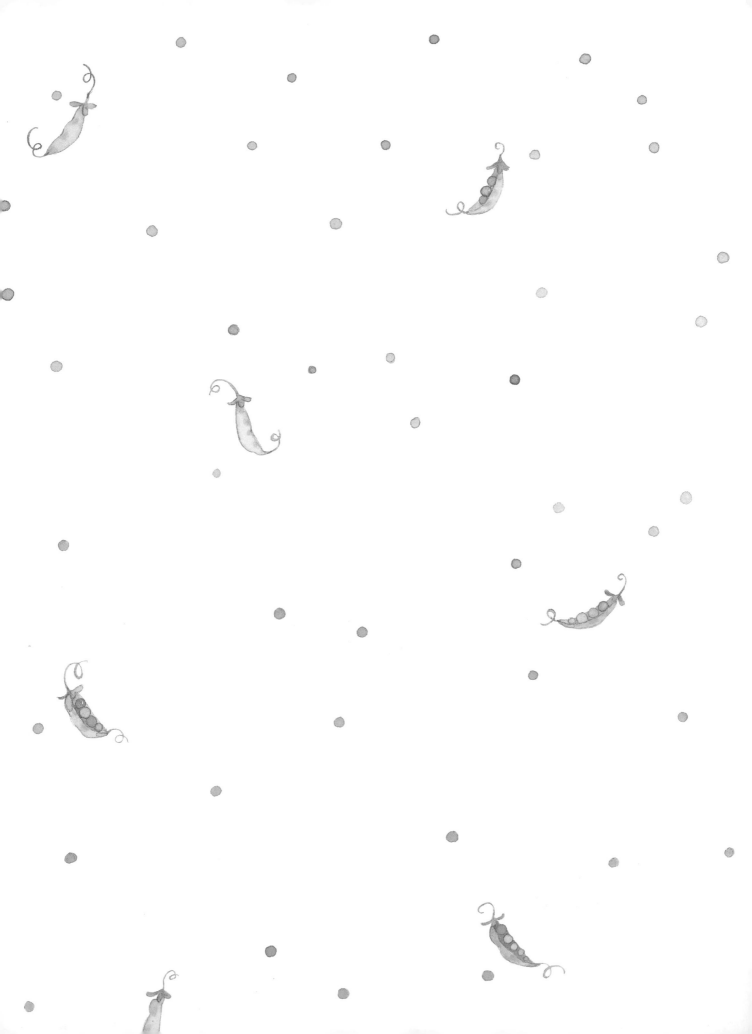

For Mom and Dad
—MGD

To Johnathon, Joey, Katelyn, Daniel
and Olivia Couri, with love
—KC

Text copyright © 2006 by Mary Delaney
Illustrations copyright © 2006 by Kathy Couri

Little, Brown and Company

Time Warner Book Group
1271 Avenue of the Americas, New York, NY 10020
Visit our Web site at www.lb-kids.com

First Edition: March 2006

Library of Congress Cataloging-in-Publication Data
Delaney, Mary
Mabel O'Leary put peas in her ear-y / by Mary Delaney; illustrated by Kathy Couri— 1st ed.
p. cm.
Summary: Hoping to avoid eating her peas, Mabel puts them in her ears
and discovers that her impaired hearing leads to other problems.
ISBN 0-316-13506-2
[1. Food habits—Fiction. 2. Peas—Fiction. 3. Stories in rhyme.]
I. Couri, Kathryn A., ill. II. Title

10 9 8 7 6 5 4 3 2 1

PHX

Printed in China

The illustrations for this book were done in watercolor and watercolor pencil
on Rives watercolor paper.

The author would like to make it clear-y:
DO NOT put any peas in your ear-y.

Mabel O'Leary Put Peas in Her Ear-y

written by Mary G. Delaney

illustrated by Kathy Couri

LITTLE, BROWN AND COMPANY
New York ⚬ Boston

Mabel O'Leary
was growing quite weary
of staring alone at her food.
Said Mother to Mabel,
"You'll sit at that table
until every pea has been chewed."

Then Mother walked out, leaving Mabel to pout and to ponder her peas and their fate.

But Mabel was wise
and soon she devised
a method for
cleaning her plate!

Now Mabel O'Leary
with tune bright and cheery
deposited peas in her ears.

She continued to hum
'til the job was all done
and every
last pea
disappeared.

Mabel's mother came in,
on her face spread a grin
when she saw that the peas were all gone.
Said Mother to Mabel, "I'm glad you were able
to finish your food before dawn."

Now Mabel jumped down
and went running around
much to her mother's dismay.
With a tone of disgust
she said, "Mabel you must
behave in a civilized way!"

But peas in the ear
make it tricky to hear,
as Mabel discovered that day.
Words seem confusing,
their meanings amusing,
ideas become hard to convey.

Mother yelled, "STOP!"
But Mabel heard "HOP!"
Which seemed like
an odd thing to say.
But wanting to please her
she tried to appease her
by hopping and yelling "Olé!"

"MABEL, HOLD STILL!"
"Get out my old drill?"
Mabel felt joy in her heart!
She emerged from
the cellar,
excited to tell her,
"I found it!
Now where do I start?"

"MABEL, YOUR MANNERS!"
"Now get me some hammers?
Okay! Should I get nails too?"
Knocking over some chairs,
she raced for the stairs,
thinking, *This is too good to be true.*

"PUT THOSE TOOLS DOWN!"
"Paint my face like a clown?"
Mom sure knows how to have fun.
She was a big bore,
but not anymore!
Now we have fun by the ton!

"YOU'RE MAKING A MESS!"
"Let's make a headdress?
Okay, let me just find my feathers."
As she dug through her drawer
Mabel yelled through the door,
"I just love doing
projects together!"

"MABEL, I MEAN IT!"
"You want me to clean it?
This floor could use
a good mopping."
She ran for detergent,
her mission was urgent,
and soon soap and water
were
slopping.

"THIS FLOOR IS ALL WET!"
"Let's sing a duet?
I'll play along on my cello."
She wailed and yowled
and warbled and howled
and screeched,
"She's a
jolly good fellow!"

Ooohhh Ooooohhh

Mabel's mouth opened wide,
then she yawned and she sighed
and she put down her cello and bow.
"This quality time
has been really divine,
but bed is where I need to go."

When she leaped into bed
Mabel tilted her head
so the peas that had muffled her hearing
started rolling around,
heading straight for the ground,
and soon they began reappearing.

As she kissed her goodnight
in the pale moonlight
Mother noticed the bed was all lumpy.
She pulled back the cover,
surprised to discover,
hundreds of peas,
green and plumpy.

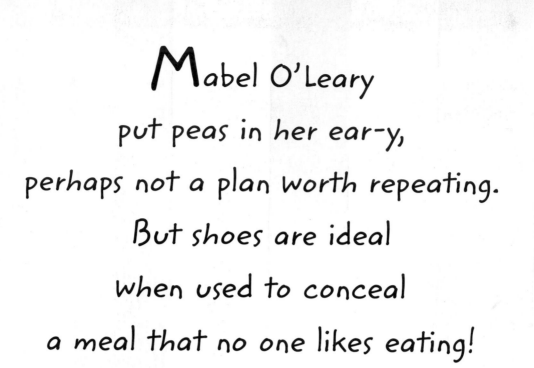

Mabel O'Leary
put peas in her ear-y,
perhaps not a plan worth repeating.
But shoes are ideal
when used to conceal
a meal that no one likes eating!